Letting Go

Letting Go

CARIE STRAWE

Art by Casey Reanna
Cover design by Ivica Jandrijevic
Interior layout and design by www.writingnights.org
Book preparation by Chad Robertson
Edited by Chad Robertson

ISBN: 978-1-7374603-2-9
Library of Congress Cataloging-in-publication Data:
Names: Strawe, Carie., author
Title: Letting Go / Carie Strawe
Description: Kintsukuroi Press, California, 2021
Identifiers: ISBN 978-1-7374603-2-9 (Perfect bound) |
978-1-7374603-0-5 (eBook)
Subjects: | Poetry | Black People | Love | Self-discovery|
Classification: Pending
LC record pending

Published by Kintsukuroi Press
Printed in the United States of America.
Printed on acid-free paper.

24 23 22 21 20 19 18 17 8 7 6 5 4 3 2 1

to you
you mean so very much to me
you know who you are
thank you for your encouragement
thank you for your love
thank you even for the pain
the exploration of self that has happened for me
was in large part due to your revealing of
your whole self to me
and for that trust, that openness
and even the tears
i am forever grateful

contents

thank you

…to those who have loved me, lost me, hurt me, nurtured me, and emboldened me. those that made me laugh, made me cry, made me mad, made me doubt myself, and made me sure of myself. to those that have wished me well and otherwise. i love each of you for helping me to grow. each level required a new me and each situation helped me to become what was needed for that next step up. the tears, the laughter, the insecurities, the overcoming, and the becoming. every second was worth it to be who i am today.

…to my amazing artist, casey reanna. my little sister. who would have known the years and the universe would bring us back together again like this? you took my words and created some of the most beautiful art i have ever seen. i could not have imagined it being done any better! this was meant to be. thank you for being open and willing. thank you for following your heart. most of all, thank you for embodying the true meaning of letting go.

x

to purchase art from casey email her at

caseyreanna@gmail.com.

to you, the reader

thank you. thank you for taking a chance on me, on my work. thank you for "listening" as i pour out my heart and soul, share my dirty little thoughts, and speak my truth. i do hope that in the pages that follow you see a little of yourself. that you can identify with the love, loss, lust, finding self-worth, and the myriad of emotions you might experience on this journey with me. i am beyond grateful for your trust in me.

now, let go.

—carie

meet carie strawe

who is carie strawe? you are. she is. he is. we are all carie strawe.

anyone who wants to be free of the constraints of the judgments of others, the judgments we often levy on ourselves.

for those who wake up in the morning and look in the mirror and say

"hell yeah, i am a sexy mofo." while your hair is everywhere, your eyes are puffy and that breath!

you, my friend, are carie strawe. the soccer moms and dads, the single parent, the single person in the midst of all of their married and kid having friends. the one who has those wild, dirty, crazy thoughts. yep, you, you little fabulous freak. the flirt, the introvert, the extrovert, the bad girls and boys, and oh yes the "good" ones too. those that enjoy pushing the limits, having the kinky sex, being wild and crazy, and sitting up front at church after it all. sensual. freaky. fun. wild. tame. loud. calm. quiet.

you. are. carie. strawe.

letting go...

of past mistakes
of shame and guilt
of not being who you were meant to be
of his lies (he didn't deserve you)
to trust… again
of other people's opinions and judgments
of her bullshit (you deserve better)
of always being a people pleaser and never a self-pleaser
of being afraid
to step out on faith
of the excuses and procrastination
of the good to get the great
of fear
to love
of the old for the new
of trying to fit in (let your freak flag fly)
of hurting yourself, hurting others
of the expectations of others
of that one that you love but doesn't love you

of whatever bullshit that is holding you back
letting go opens you to receive more.
it may be painful at first
stretching, growing, overcoming, and becoming always
is
but on the other side of it you will say that wasn't so
bad
and wonder why you didn't do it sooner

    let. go.

Beautiful

his name for me is Beautiful....
oddly enough that's also what his Love is
so beautiful in fact i am willing to risk all that i have

for the exhilarating sensation of his illicit Love.
distance, time and circumstances separate us
it pains me to be without him
my heart aches to be near him
we refuse to listen to reason and go our separate ways
but isn't love itself an unreasonable emotion?

how much longer will we continue
to punish ourselves for the sake of Love?
phone calls, webcams, letters, emails, text messages...
anything that will erase the distance
how can a love that is so improbable be so perfect?
how can two people that can't seem to physically get
near each other
have an emotional and mental bond closer than any
other

ever had between two people?

the impossibility of it all is remarkable, what's even more

is the fact that we continue to make it work.

but hasn't love always been an unfathomable thing?

his name for me is Beautiful....

oddly enough, so is the Love that we share.

so beautiful in fact we are willing to risk all that we have to keep it.

mind reader

often women want men to be mind readers
we want them to know what we are thinking
and just act upon it
while that sounds great in theory
i have come to realize that women who want that
just do not realize what they asking for
this man of mine he does this
he reads my mind
well he calls it being in tune or reading my energy
i will allude to something and he will say,
"yeah. because you feel this way about it"
"i never told you that. why would you assume?" i say
"babe, i am not blind. i can see it."
he then proceeds to tell how he knows
what he has said is true, and the problem is
he is usually right and it is so aggravating
he knows things before i want to express them to him
while this can be aggravating it is more of a blessing
to have a man that is so in tune with me that
he knows how i am feeling and is willing to express

his thoughts and be sensitive to mine at the same time

he lovingly calls me out when i try to mask my feelings

encouraging me to own them and be comfortable

with who i am and how i feel in various situations

often women want men to be mind readers

we want them to know what we are thinking

and just act upon it

while that sounds great in theory

if you ever get a man like this

and know that they are quite rare

you better be ready to own your feelings

be willing to be open and honest in every situation

there will be no hiding from this

man that can read your mind, your energy, and your

heart

Black don't crack

Black don't crack
is an old adage that i have heard my whole life
and quite honestly...it's true
most black men and women barely age and when they
do
it's done so gracefully that you often question if it really
happened

Black don't crack
for the grandmother that is out with her grandbabies
and she is mistaken for their mother

Black don't crack for the man with his son
and is mistaken for his big brother

Black don't crack for me having a conversation
with a white woman who was giving me her "sage
advice"
saying that many young ladies like me will wish we had
taken

better care of our skin by the time we reach her age
(mid-40s she told me)
my response: lady i am 42 years old, but thanks for the
advice

Black don't crack... until it does

Black don't crack until it's being followed around a
convenience store
because a large Black man is clearly a threat for no
other reason
than he is a large Black man

Black don't crack until it's pulled over by an
overzealous cop who has
absolutely no excuse to overreact except for,
you know,
he feared for his life,

because she had the audacity to ask, "why am i being
pulled over?"

Black don't crack until it's walking home late one night
minding its own business
but someone deems him "sketchy" looking...
there goes another crack.

when Black does crack, the sound is one that has
reverberated through centuries
fissures that have yet to be corrected, fixed, or filled in.
when Black cracks those crevices release the wretched
sounds
of slavery, jim crow, lynchings, segregation, and racism
the sounds of bombs over tulsa, rosewood, the tearing
down of Black culture.

the creation of these cracks has become commonplace
but a warning to those that continue to perpetuate
these foundational errors
you will pay for your deeds and those cracks will
eventually swallow you whole

the chase

he is drawn to her before he even knows she is in the
room
she senses his presence
the silent meeting. eye contact.
the exchange of slight smiles.
another chance meeting.
mutual attraction. words exchanged.
he is impressed with her.
her smile, her mind, her speech.
she is drawn to him.
his gentle demeanor, his good looks.
    it begins.

she makes the first move, amazing him further.
invitation to dinner
she is honest and beautiful.
he is drawn in.
he is sensitive and a gentleman.
she is fascinated.

it continues.
a night of drinks and dancing.
she moves in a way that
takes his thoughts to another place
she is sensual, sexy, unequivocally stunning.
the restraint.

he struggles to control his reaction to her.
she skirts the line of no return.
it happens.
the kiss, the line is crossed.
and so it begins…

his essence

the thought of you in my mind
makes me want
the taste of you on my tongue
the smell of you in my nostrils
the sound of your voice in my ears
and the weight of you on top of me

the answer

you wanted to know what i would do to you when i get
the opportunity to be alone with you. well, here is the
answer...
i would first resume the kiss we started so many
months ago
that kiss has been haunting me since that day
it was perfect except for the fact that it had to end
i believe lovemaking begins well before you reach
the bed and that foreplay is a constant state of mind
i would take my time kissing you, looking into your
eyes,
telling you how much i love you without saying a word
as much as i love words and what they can convey, i
believe
they would only get in the way of this moment
we have done nothing but talk up to now. what more
would there be to say?
i would feed you (chocolate covered fruit maybe?)
as clothing is removed little by little
i would cover you with kisses exploring every

unclothed part of you with my lips and my tongue

i want to take you between my lips and feel how hard i

make you.

i want to run my tongue from tip to bottom. i want to

feel you throb in my mouth

we would eventually end up in bed (or wherever) and i

would welcome you gladly to all that is inside of me

any way you want it

i want to wrap my legs around you and feel every inch

of you in me

i want you to feel what has been craving you

the warmth, the wetness, the softness...all of it

i want to give to you all that i have to offer emotionally,

mentally, physically

that kiss

have you ever been kissed in a way that
made you feel like you had never been kissed before?
this is what that kiss was
that kiss was what you see in movies
but never really believed it was real
long text message conversations
a few phone calls
all leading to the moment of that kiss
he came over
we both had other engagements but
made time to get together
we sat and talked
the kind of conversation where one
begins to truly tell you who they are
revealing. deep. honest.
mixed with a little laughter here and there
lingering until the last moment
walking him to the door i could
sense his hesitation but feel his energy

in it was the desire to explore
ever the gentleman, not wanting to
come on too strong he was cautious
watching waiting for the invitation
i on the other hand had already walked
through this in my mind
if he hesitates
i wont

at the door he mentions something i said in a prior
conversation
"so, you can figure out a person in a matter of a couple
of minutes," he says
and there it is
"yes, i can," i respond
"well i must see this," he says
his voice sends waves through me
those eyes that perfect smile
his cologne is absolutely intoxicating, heady

yes you must
my hand on his side giving a slight nudge in my direction
my body is pressed against his now
there is an inviting softness amidst all those muscles
i breathe him in
in my head alarms are going off

oh shit! it's happening.
that kiss

my lips press against his
perfectly soft.
immediately i am lost in him

his hand touches the side of my face
such a sensual act
that does something to me
the other arm around my waist
the strength of him
i almost feel like i'm off my feet
his kiss is absolute perfection
just enough tongue action to make
me want more of it

his light moan told me that
he had been waiting just as i had for this moment
sade's "no ordinary love" playing in the background
we are at the door, a tangle of arms, lips and tongues
it was then that i realized my foot was up
after what felt like quite some time, but still not
quite long enough
we slowly lean back from each other
looking into each other's eyes there was really no need

for words
we smile and not having had enough we kiss more

at the point now where we both must go
reluctantly we separate
"i look forward to more of this and you as soon as
possible," he says
barely breathing at this point i tell him only if he
promises not to behave
he agrees. we laugh, hug, another quick kiss and he
leaves
i close the door, lean against it, close my eyes and
breathe deep
i can still smell him on me. still feel his hand on my face
and the weight of him against me
immediately i miss him
damn
that kiss

colorful dreams

i dreamed of you last night
i dreamed in color
there were blue skies above us
green grass beneath our feet
your beautifully brown eyes and dazzling white smile
set against mahogany dark skin
my heart raced when you touched me
flushing my honey caramel cheeks
a deep shade of pink
chocolate kisses on my sun bronzed skin
launch the flight of yellow orange and
purple butterflies that flutter in my stomach
sunlight pales in comparison to the glow i give
when you tell me you Love me…
it was all so real i fought to stay asleep
never wanting it to end
the winds begin to blow, gray clouds move in
covering our sun
the sky darkens turning
pitch black our beautiful green grass

turns a lifeless brown

i try to hold on with everything in me

i reach for you in the shadows but you are

no longer there

the alarm blares

opening my eyes to reality

black and gray are my days

but when i dream i dream in color

  i dream of you

the getaway

no one knows who we are
that we don't belong to each other
we walk hand in hand laughing
Loving
among crowds of blank faces
we feel free fearless alive
unseen by the eyes that are all around us
we have only a short time to pretend
we meet in a random city
where we have no ties
for that time we live for and love only each other
forgetting the lives we left behind
when our time comes to an end
we return to our separate realities
holding on to the private memories
we share only with each other
and the anticipation of the time to come
the next getaway

the show

across the room you sit. naked.
in a chair with a perfect view of the bed
i walk in. killer high heels, thigh high stockings, garter.

standing in front of you, i lean over with only a couple
of inches
between my lips and yours. i explain the rules:
you stay in the chair. you can do whatever you want
but you stay in the chair. understand?
you steal a quick kiss and answer, "yes dear."

i roll my eyes and grin as i slowly saunter over to my
playground
on the bed i am surrounded by toys.
dildos of different textures, colors, and sizes
silicone. glass. metal. vibrating. thrusters.
vibrating remote controlled bullets.
anal plugs and toys of varying sizes.

sexy, slow music plays in the background

i grab a medium sized anal plug with a red gemstone
on the end
i lick it, lube it up, and with my ass in full view of you
slowly slide it inside me. playing with my ass.
moaning and grinning i look over at you.
already you are positioned: dick in hand
on my back now legs wide open
knees up with my red gemstone sparkling at you
i reach for a deep purple twisted glass dildo
i hear you moan in agreement with my choice
sliding it inside me i feel the coolness
it makes my breath catch

i lick my lips, bite my bottom lip, and push it further
it syncs with my body temperature as the friction of
me sliding it in and out increases
the twisted glass gives my pussy sensations that
are seen in the shifting of my hips
and vocalized in my moans of shits and damns
i start to remove it and from across the room you say

"no. keep going."
i flash a look at you of potential defiance but
obey your command and keep going
slowly in and slowly out as you stroke your dick to the
same rhythm

faster you tell me and i oblige
moving the twisted glass faster i can feel
my body is starting to give in

"yes" escapes my lips as i hear "no" from yours
what?!
"no," you say. "you may not cum yet. not until i say so."
the grin on your face says quite clearly that
payback is a dirty little bitch
touché my love, well played
slowly i remove the glass dildo and reach for a different
toy
this one a larger jet-black dildo that reminds me of you

your smile tells me you already know that
i lick the entire length of it with my tongue all the way
out
i suck on it like it's you. i gag on it
you start to move
"nope. stay in the chair. i told you."
your frustration is so sexy
the power button sends the toy thrusting and rotating
at the same time
the arrows go through various levels of vibrations
i tease my clit. the vibrations are intense
inside me the thrusting rotation and vibrations

are such an extreme combination that it immediately
sends my body into light convulsions

"fuck," i yell
as i hear you say "i did not tell you that you could cum
yet."
"please," i beg as i feel my body being pulled to the edge
of the bed
holding the chair to you, you have walked to the edge
of the bed
removing the toy from me and positioning me on top
of you to ride your dick
you look at me and say, "now you can cum."

legs wrapped around you, slowly riding you, it turns
faster,
more primitive as your moans turn into light growls
my nipples in your mouth, your hands gripping my ass
my fingers digging into your back
your dick inside me is rubbing against the anal plug
i moan loudly
and that sensation along with all the others
forces a release from my body
"give it to me" you tell me
as we cum together
breathing heavy, completely spent from the teasing

and now sudden, sodden, release of tension
we melt into each other
i whisper in your ear, "did you enjoy the show?"
your response: "nope i want my money back. you
didn't even use all the toys!"
laughter. fun. love.

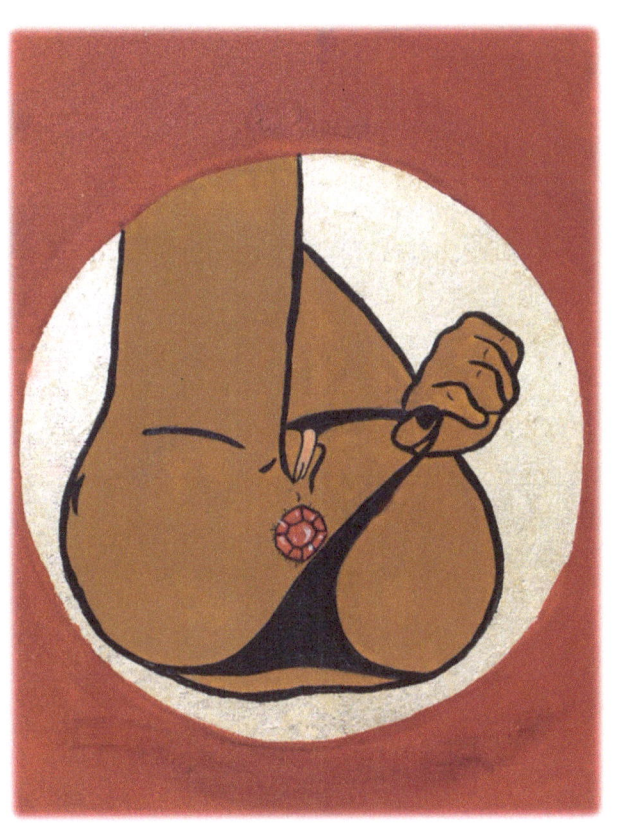

forever/right now

forever? nothing lasts forever

you and i are not lost on that fact

we know that at some point this will end

i dont know when that time will be or

the circumstances that will bring it to pass

what i do know is this

i Love you right now

right now i want nothing more than to make you happy

right now i Love this

     us

what we are to each other

right now i want you, need you, and can't stand to be away from you.

right now the thought of you makes me smile

hearing your voice makes my heart skip a beat

and seeing your face takes my breath away

     all i want is right now

in bed alone

lying in bed alone... thoughts of you
wishing you were beside me. missing you.
the mere thought of your voice incites a
smoldering flame that heats my body from the inside
out
remembering your touch gives way
to flutters deep inside me. my fingers fan the flames.
closing my eyes and reliving the last time i
felt you explore the depths of my soul... a light moan
of remembrance escapes from my throat
my body arches, muscle memory, searching
for the perfect fit it feels every time it's
up against yours my hips move to the
melodious rhythm our bodies make together...
your breath, then mine, your whispers in my ear
my gasp for air as you push deep inside me... a Love
symphony.
i am there with you, i can smell your scent, feel your
arms
around me pulling me into you, your kiss

i can feel the all too familiar tingles signaling my climax
you push deeper, you tell me you Love me, my body
responds by releasing all that it's holding to you...
i open my eyes to find that i am
lying in bed alone... thoughts of you
wishing you were beside me. missing you.

eyes wide shut

when i close my eyes....
i take a breath and i smell your scent
i can see your face, your smile, those eyes that make my
heart melt
i feel your hand on mine
our fingers interlaced
i see a chocolate sea of limbs entangled in seductive,
sensual passion
my body responds willingly to your every unspoken
command
in darkness we navigate each other's bodies
not by sight but memory
my breath catches as you enter me
we move as one because that is what we have become
i hear your voice moaning in my ear
my legs wrapped around your waist,
my hands grip your back
our contrasting tones attempt to show
where one ends and the other begins
but to no avail

i feel your breath on my neck
i moan your name
your body responds to my call
growing harder, moving deeper
a melodious rhythm that only the symphony
of our two bodies can make, fills the room....
my eyes open
i take a breath and i smell your scent
and await the next time that i get to

    close my eyes

center of attention

i had been so curious for so long. a number of people i know would talk about it.

what was it really like? it just seems like there would be too much going on. confusing maybe?

i wanted to know for myself. but how? he wanted it too though.

he wanted me to experience it, but even more he wanted to watch me with someone else.

initially i thought that was odd, but it would give us both what we want.

we have always been completely open to experiencing pleasure on whatever level.

no judgment, was our thing. if it brings you pleasure, ask for it. if it can be done, we do it.

we toyed with the idea before, but it was never a serious conversation.

not until i made it one, late one night.

"babe, you ever had a threesome?" i asked.

"yes," he answered. "you knew that though."

"yes you told me, but you never told me details."

"why do you want details?" he asks.

"i just want to know what it's like," i tell him.

"well you should explore that... we should explore that," he says with a huge grin.

"my rules," i told him.

he agreed.

"the other has to be someone i do not know but you know and trust. someone who has just as much to lose as we do, if not more. "

he agreed.

"i make all final decisions."

he agreed again.

i believe he would have agreed to nearly anything i said to see this finally happen.

so now here we are.

he had someone in mind, showed me a picture.

he knows my type for sure.

chocolate skin, great smile, muscles, overall good looking.

we spoke on the phone. it was casual conversation like you would have when getting to know someone you just met and may want to go out with. he was funny, easy to talk to, flirty but respectful. he was perfect. we set a date.

day of driving to the hotel and my guy asks me, "you nervous?"
"no. not really," i answered. "i honestly just want it to live up to the hype."
he laughed.

our guest was due to arrive at the hotel in a couple of hours. he gets showered and goes downstairs to wait, giving me time to relax.
with slow, sexy music playing, candles lit, i take a long hot shower.

lotioned, very little makeup, my kinky twists are the perfect style for this little venture.
black, lace cheeky panties and black high heels. i feel extremely sexy and cannot wait to be seen.

i send main a mirror selfie. he is at the door a couple minutes later. tells me that guest is about fifteen minutes out but he wanted to get things started.
fondling me, kissing me all over, teasing me. at this point i am so turned on.

knock at the door.

"wait," i tell him. "one more thing."

i reach over and grab a black, satin blindfold and lie down on the bed. the blindfold is sexy and bestows a little mystery, but it is honestly more of a safety net for me.

main kisses my cheek, whispers in my ear how sexy i am and thanks me for giving him this gift. he goes to the door.

i hear the door open.

they exchange hellos.

main tells guest that all is set and once he gets out of the shower, it's on. i am a little anxious.

i hear the shower go on and then off a few minutes later. it wasn't long, but felt like it.

main whispers in my ear, "you control this. this is your show. i will never be out of reach."

he kisses me deep, caresses my face.

then i hear a somewhat familiar voice. "damn you are so sexy."

my assumption is that he is standing at the foot of the bed taking me in. i smile.

"come here," i tell him. i reach my hand out for him, he

takes hold of and kisses it.

i pull him to me, kiss him deeply, and then i whisper, "do with me what you will. let's see if you can handle it."

immediately there were hands. hands all over me.

i was being kissed, and my thigh rubbed on by main. guest was fingering my pussy and sucking on my nipples. being blindfolded, i was surprised by every touch, every kiss.

all my other senses were beyond heightened and sent into overdrive.

for a split second it was oddly disorienting.

i could not make sense of what was happening or what i was feeling.

then i realized, they are here for me. their sole purpose was to pleasure me.

i was the center of attention. this is my show to run.

in that moment, this feeling of absolute euphoria came over me. i felt amazingly sexy. desired.

i pushed guest's head down, and told him to taste me. obediently his mouth devoured my pussy. i attempted to move, but those muscles held me in place. main is kissing and rubbing all over me. the constant touching is feeding this feeling that has now taken control of me.

"feed me," i tell main.

"gladly," he answers. guest is feasting on me and moaning in delight. on his knees beside me, main slides his dick into my mouth. his hand in my hair turns me on. i control the motion. he moans. the sounds can only be described as an orchestra of absolute pleasure. the three of us are enjoying our current roles and waiting for my cue to change up. i give it.

i tell guest that i want to feel him deep inside me. dutifully he answers, "anything you wish sexy."

i felt him over me. wrapped my leg around him, bringing him closer to me as he slid inside. he moaned deep. my breath catches. his dick fills me. he is thick and just long enough that an, "oh shit," escapes my lips. he grabs my left leg and puts it on his shoulder. then he kisses me deep. i did not expect that but welcomed it. i taste amazing on his lips and i tell him so. he says, "you taste amazing. period." main, as promised, is within reach. i feel him holding my right hand and kissing my neck. he whispers in my ear how amazing i look.

i feel amazing right now as guest continues to push deep in me in a slow, steady motion.

he is giving me the perfect fucking to lovemaking ratio.

he is gentle but so damn strong.

he knows what he is doing and i am loving it. both arms wrapped around him now, my left hand behind his head, my right hand gripping his back and running across the flexing muscles in his arm. main lets me know he is there when i feel his hand caress my right leg. my hips move with guest, pushing against him, i hear him moan, "fuck yes baby. give it to me. damn you are so fucking perfect. this pussy is perfect."

"you're welcome," i tell him. "show me how perfect it is." he pushes even deeper into me and puts my nipple in his mouth. that pushes me over the edge. i push in to him even more. i feel myself about to cum. he must feel it as well. my pussy is squeezing his dick and i feel him pulsing. i can't stop it and i start to cum just as he begins to give a low growl and cums with me.

"what the fuck!" he says. "i have never cum that fast."

"you've never been with me," i snap back. we all laugh.

i tell him i want to taste me on him.
he lies down.

i am now on my hands and knees between his legs. i take my time and lick him from balls to tip. kissing every inch slowly and purposefully. taking him in my mouth deeply. to the point of choking a little. he shifts. "damn," he yells. i smile. i feel his hand on the side of my face, holding it for a beat. i believe he is just looking at me.

"you are one sexy ass woman."

"thank you," i say.

i hear main say, "yes, she is," as his hand smacks my ass turned up in the air. i suck guest's dick deep again. i feel main's mouth on my pussy from behind. again the orchestra. in full swing again. moans and the noises that only damn good sex can create.

main's mouth gives way to his dick.

the surprise of it makes me gasp. as i continue to suck guest's dick, the feeling is indescribable.

in comparison to guest's, main's dick is not quite as thick but plenty long and the access he has in this position allows him to penetrate me so deep. loving every moment of this i have little time to think about what comes next. i just do what i feel. once main and i cum with him behind me, guest is rock hard again and i want to ride him, so i do. i slide on top of his dick and he immediately grabs my hips as i expertly lift myself up and down on him, grinding at the right times to feel every inch of him deep in me. leaning over him, i put my titties in his face and he, knowing exactly what to do, goes licking and sucking from one to the other sending me into convulsions. my pussy gripping him sends him over the edge. he grabs my hips and pushes me deeper into him. breathing heavy we both are just there for a moment. as he puts his hand on my face again and caresses it. i move to lay next to him. i feel main behind me. sandwiched between these two men again gives rise to the sexy-desired feelings. they are both kissing and touching all over me. it is such an intoxicating feeling to be the center of so much sexual energy. feeling completely comfortable and realizing how odd it must be for me to still be blindfolded, i take the blindfold off. guest looks even better than his picture. he is looking at me and seems at a bit of a loss for words for a second. then he says, "you are absolutely beautiful."

"thank you. you are damn good looking yourself," i tell him. i feel him get hard against me. not ready to end things just yet, i turn to main, get on my knees and start sucking his dick. he is loving it. i stop just long enough to tell guest, "don't be shy. you are welcome to join us." his tongue shocks me as it enters my pussy. he's licking my pussy and eating my ass as if he is starved. i continue to suck main. he watches me, and i am looking up at him. with his hand in my hair, he quietly asks, "are you happy?" just as guest slides his dick in me. "yes," i moan in response to them both.

guest is sliding in and out of me, smacking my ass and moaning as i continue to make main moan by making his dick disappear in my mouth. it was a beautiful feeling to be getting pleased by and to be giving pleasure to them both.

they are done. even though i could have gone again.

laying there with them, a tangle of limbs, both of them pressed against me, i think of how the night could not have gone any better. so much so that i am already thinking of the next time i get to be the center of attention.

scaling the libra

he is Beautiful.
known for good looks, he does not disappoint
perfectly shaped full lips that can, without warning,
release a gorgeous smile that reflects his nearby sun
eyes like dark piercing diamonds they look deep into
my soul
there is no hiding from him
he is sensitive.

he has a softness that makes me want to open up to him
he watches intently as i shed my shell
sharing things that most will never know about me
he rewards this by making himself vulnerable
he speaks of the things that matter most to him
wholly revealing himself, showing that there are no
pretenses, no games.

the door of his seventh house opens, welcoming me
his air element surrounds me.
i breathe him in. slowly. deeply.

with a reigning venus, his sexual intuition is beyond
heightened.
he responds to my every silent request. my body
communicating to him
in a language that only he understands and i didn't
even know i spoke.

sharing the cardinal quality,
a seductive struggle for sensual jurisdiction ensues.
not one for conflict, the libran concedes
but only to achieve the balance it craves
my luminous moon eclipses, shining fully on us both.

my water element mixed with his air creates a
shortness of breath
the stars witness the colliding of two planets that were
to never touch
madly fascinated with each other
there is an undeniable cosmic allure
sadly, the constellations will not allow our union
see, the fluidity i possess will never meet his innate
need for balance.

we continue to orbit, passing each other briefly
remembering when for a fleeting moment
venus and the moon became one.

the misconception: a chat with my Queen sisters

what is really going on with the misconception of Black hair?

a true Queen can wear any crown.

it does not matter if it is curly, kinky, short, nappy, wavy, long, bone straight, dyed, twisted, or tied.

It is all Beautiful, because you are all Beautiful.

the freedom we possess to do the most amazing things with our tresses

is envied the world over.

it is said that imitation is the best compliment…and imitate us, they do!

when we wear cornrows, it is ghetto. let others do it and it is now a fashionable trend.

when we wear weave in its many forms it is considered deceitful or fake. when others do it is simply adding variety to their hairstyle options.

our natural hair is looked at as unkempt and unprofessional. others' natural hair is pointed to as the standard we should aspire to.

we are descendants of Queens who beautifully adorned their intricately braided hair with the finest of jewels and gold.

now there are those who will attempt to shame us while showing their ignorance of our royal status with silly things they say like, "what did you do to your hair? i liked it better the way you had it before. why can't you just wear your hair normal? what do you do to get it to look like that? let's not forget my personal favorite, "is that your hair?"

Queens! do not trouble yourself with those who refuse to recognize your royal splendor.
let us hold our heads high as the royalty we indeed are.
wear your crown with an attitude and grace that would do madame c. j. walker proud.

see, the real misconception is that many have missed the concept of Black being beautiful.
most have absolutely missed the notion that their
issue with my hair is not about me at all, but completely about them

their discomfort with my complete comfortability
with who and how i was made
it bothers them. the audacity of me walking into this
space, back straight, head held high
rocking this crown that was handed down through
generations of struggle, through centuries of oppression,
through decades of attempting to be straightened out.
well i do hope that they are well prepared to get
comfortable with
being uncomfortable for quite a long time
because i will not drop the mantle entrusted to me by
so many.
i will not bow to those who see me as inferior. and

why would i?

what's a mob to Queen? royalty does not lose sleep
over those that have no power to dethrone.
heavy is the head that wears this crown.
    thank God He built me for it

why....

(a message to a young girl)

why are you the one to sacrifice for others?
when will they sacrifice anything for you?
why must you be the one to bend over backwards
to make them happy?
have they ever made that effort for you?
why do you constantly feel the need to make
yourself small in their presence?
when will you figure out that they are the small ones
that
possess small minds that cannot begin to fathom the
enormity of you?
when will you realize your worth?
you are so much more than what you give yourself
credit for
why do you entertain those who cannot see that?
why do you not see it?
people can only treat you the way you allow them to
the way you treat yourself
if you do not value you, neither will they

you are so much more than the sum of your parts
you are unique, talented, intelligent, loving and
absolutely beautiful on the inside as well as the outside
you must insist on being loved from the inside out
not the other way around

two sides

hers—

saying goodbye is the hardest thing to do... for some i
guess

you did it so effortlessly. the words just flowed easily...
"i can't do this anymore."

as i sat there, my heart breaking was the loudest sound
in my ears

is that why it's called a breakup? has to be

did you even hear it?

it was louder than the rain. louder than your
explanation of why

louder than my empty words to you

"ok. i understand."

why did i say that?

no the fuck i don't understand!

i don't understand this at all

as i got out the car he got out. why? dammit i just
wanted to walk away.

he hugged me. fuck! really? i get lost in his hugs. i hear
him say, "i am sorry."

you should be. that's what i should have said. instead i say, "don't be."

why did i say that? you damn right you are sorry! you will never find another me.

all i wanted was you. us. i wanted to give you everything.

actually that's wrong. all i want is you. us. i want to give you everything.

it's not past tense. that is the stupid thing. i still want to be with you

the pain in my chest is saying otherwise, but i am so lost in you

that i will ignore it

if you were to walk back through that door to me i would forgive all.

   we could be happy.

why can't you just see me instead of the issue?

   it's not that you can't, you won't.

his—

it was the hardest thing sitting in that car in the rain

her sitting there listening to me, looking into me the way she does

she has to know something is off

fuck! how do i say this?

then there it was. i said it damn near without even

realizing it

but that look on her face told me that i did

she is such an amazing woman

i just can't get past it though. it's hard. to be honest, i
am scared.

as i explained she just sat there

she said she understood but does she?

does she know that i have never really trusted anyone
like i have her

that i have never opened up as much to anyone

i felt like an asshole sitting there watching her be the
strong woman she is

she said ok. she got out. i got out. as i hugged her and
said i was sorry she simply said,

"don't be." and then she was gone. she didn't even look

back.

    i wish i could get past it but i just can't.

the impression

your kisses cannot be forgotten, for my lips won't allow
it
i will forever long for the softness of your touch
the ecstasy my body has experienced by your hand
time after time
is indelibly inscribed into my memories
your lips move across my skin leaving gentle promises
to return
your tongue leaves a trail of breathless shivers in its
wake
our bodies fit together like interlocking puzzle pieces
that have always created an intensely erotic scene:
desire meeting passion
        perfect. beautiful. amazing.

you are worthy

be true to you

love you first and foremost

without this your light cannot shine fully

you cannot truly love others

it all starts with self love

it starts with you

love your skin

love your hair

love your eyes

love your mind (and sharpen it daily)

love your body

listen to your laugh and love the sound of it

be comfortable and happy with you

let no one tell you that

you are not good enough

that you are not worthy

you are

you know damn well you are

now get out there and act like it

the wall (an office romance)

as silly as this may seem to you
i am sitting down the hall from where you are
but i am missing you like you are
miles away from me...

did you finish the reports that are due today?
yes, they are on the program mangers desk already

i see you many times throughout the day
but at this moment
i feel as if it's been days since i
last laid eyes on you
your smile, your touch, your kiss...

hey! did you see the game last night?
uhm, yeah i did. crazy right?

all beautiful memories
this simple wall that separates us
feels like an ocean

with you on one side and me on the other...

did you hear about the big boss and his assistant?
what? no. let's talk at lunch ok? a little busy right now.

i look at it and wonder if you are on
the other side of it
thinking of me the way i am
thinking of you right now...

good morning, this is carie with customer relations.
yes, of course i can assist you ma'am
if you would give me your first and last name i can look
that up for you...

it's such a silly thing my heart
and the things it feels for you

kintsukuroi

broken is better than new?
tell that to my heart

it has been broken so many times
that no amount of lacquer, gold or otherwise,
can bring the pieces back together
the many nights crying in my sleep
loneliness gripping me as a random he laid next to me

the constant news flashes
followed by toe tags and hashtags
the piercing words from forked tongues
that left unreachable blades in my back
the many times i stared in the mirror
trying to see the Beauty but only feeling the disdain

broken for so long and into so many pieces...

then one day, something changed

i woke up and decided to choose different

i looked in the mirror and chose
to talk to myself instead of listen to myself
i told me how proud of me i was
for getting through all the pain and hurt
for choosing to get up even when i didn't feel like it

i realized it was all a choice
while i had not chosen to be hurt by others
i had a choice in whether to stay hurt and broken
i chose not to. i chose me.
everyday i felt a little stronger, a little less broken
then one day i saw it
the golden glow that comes from mended cracks
radiating from within, drawing like energy.

so is broken better than new?
only if you choose to allow the beauty
of who you were truly meant to be
to shine through the cracks

kintsukuroi (金繕い) explained
(kint-soo-ko-roy)

kintsukuroi is a japanese art where something broken (think ceramics like pottery, bowls, cups) is repaired with gold (sometimes silver or platinum) colored lacquer. the cracks are now a part of the history of the item. the repair reveals a beauty in the brokenness. the gold streaks make the item stronger and more valuable. broken is better than new.

kintsukuroi is beautifully translated, "golden repair" and in life can teach us to celebrate our flaws and imperfections, to embrace our history instead of being ashamed of, hiding, or denying it. the breaks and resulting cracks were not the destruction of the thing, but the building and strengthening of it.

you will see this used in the cover art (and title art piece) for this book as well as the art piece for "Black don't crack." i have fully adopted kintsukuroi as a philosophy for living my life and invite you to do the same. we are all broken in some way. will you embrace the beauty in your brokenness, becoming stronger for it, more beautiful? or will you allow it to destroy you?

you have a choice.

choose wisely.

—carie

you've reached the end, dear reader. i'm sorry it's over too. thanks for reading *letting go*. i hope you loved it.

as an independent author, i count on readers like you to spread the word and support future work. if you enjoy this book, please join the ranks of my readers who make it all possible. you can:

-write a review on amazon
https://www.amazon.com/dp/B097LG66TM.

-connect on social

ig: @iamcariestrawe
fb: carie strawe

please connect, i'd love to stay in touch.

thanks again,
—carie

www.ingramcontent.com/pod-product-compliance
Lightning Source LLC
Chambersburg PA
CBHW041408010726
47507CB00001B/42